What I Am

Divya Srinivasan

VIKING

I am a girl.
I am a human.
I am a human animal.

I am a daughter.

I am a granddaughter.

I am an Amma to my guys.

I am vegetarian.

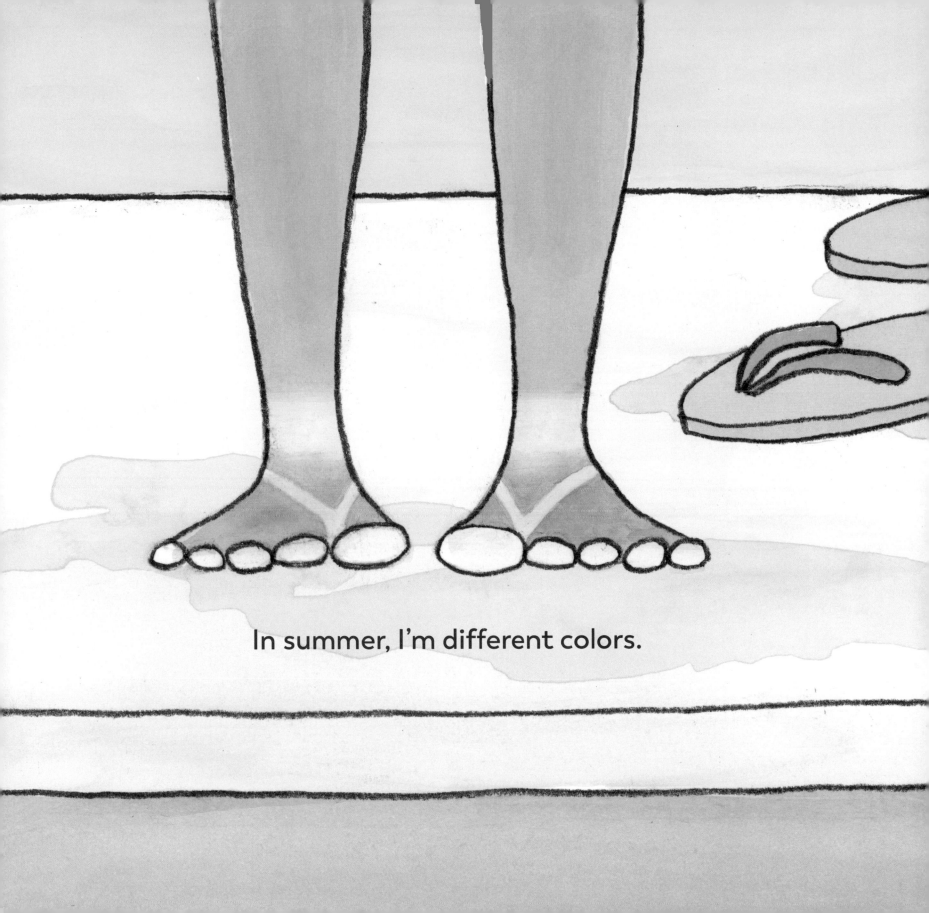

In summer, I'm different colors.

I like to look at animals,

but I am nervous around animals.

I don't win.

I love what I made!

I might be an artist.

I have so much.

I don't have enough.

I am selfish.

I am generous.

I am mean.

I am kind.

I am a scaredy-cat.

I am brave.

I am not mischievous

(most of the time).

Sometimes I am a witch!

I like to be with friends.

I like to be alone.

I dance! I sing!

I don't want to go
to parties.

Am I shy?

I say hi.

I don't want to leave
parties.

I am American.
I am Indian.

What I am
is more than I can say.

I am part of the world.
I am part of the universe.

Author's Note

Years ago, my sister was washing her hands in a restroom when a lady at the next sink looked at her and asked, "What *are* you?"

My sister was confused, but quickly figured out this stranger was asking about her race. Instead of a friendly, casual *how* are you, the question was a nosy, pointed *what* are you. As if my sister were a thing—a curiosity—and not a person. Intentional or not, the lady's words were insulting. My sister remained polite, and the lady went on her way. But the words stayed with my sister, and she called me.

We talked about how she should have responded. What if she had replied, "I am a human"? We laughed and thought of other suitable responses. "I am hungry." "I am taller than you." "I am . . . washing my hands." It felt good to laugh together about the absurd situation, but the stranger's words still weighed on us.

Our talk left me agitated, and I took a walk to calm down. I started thinking about how I would define myself. I had argued with my mother that day. "I am a rude daughter." I still hadn't returned a friend's phone call. "I am a bad friend." I ate junk food earlier. "I don't take care of myself!"

I *was* on a walk, though. "I exercise!" I was there for my sister when she needed me. "I am helpful." I bought my mother comfy slippers when she mentioned having sore feet. "I am pretty thoughtful." By the time I returned home, I had a long, unwieldy, and still incomplete list of what I am.

There are so many ways you might see yourself and see others, depending on what you focus on. No one is easily defined, and we are all so much more than what can be seen on the outside.

Recently, I thought about a child being asked such a question. My fantasy scenario goes something like this:

Rude person: What are you?

Child: I am a *who*, not a *what*.

Then the rude person leaves, feeling embarrassed, because the kid is right! I imagined the child later pondering the strange question and thinking about all that she is, and realizing in the end, "I am more than I can say."

People can be thoughtless and hurt our feelings, even if they don't mean to. Regardless of how others act, though, we must take care never to doubt our own worth. Each of us is a unique, priceless, vital part of this world.

We are all important in so many ways. We are all more than we can say.

Divya Srinivasan